Winnie the Pooh's Movie Theatre Storybook

Adapted by Merry North

Contents

Reader's
Digest
Children's Books®

Pleasantville, New York • Montréal, Québec • Bath, United Kingdom

The Many Adventures of Winnie The Pooh

Chapter 1: Pooh's Honey Tree

Winnie the Pooh was a tubby bear who lived in the Hundred-Acre Wood. One day, he was rumbly in his tumbly—time for a snack! But his honeypot was empty. A bee buzzing around his head gave Pooh an idea. He followed the bee to a honey tree and began to climb.

DISK 1
1

"Time to munch an early lunch…" he hummed. Suddenly, a branch snapped and Pooh fell into a bush. Ouch! He crawled out and went searching for his friend Christopher Robin.

Christopher Robin was busy tacking on Eeyore's tail as Kanga and little Roo watched.

"Thanks," Eeyore said gloomily. "It's not much

2 of a tail…but I'm sort of attached to it."

"Do you have a balloon?" Pooh asked Christopher Robin. In fact, he did. Pooh covered himself in mud. "I'm a little black rain cloud," he announced. "Aim me at the bees!"

3 Holding onto the balloon, muddy Pooh rose up until he reached a hole in the tree. A swarm of bees came out to investigate. They chased Pooh around the tree until all the air

4 hissed out of the balloon. Pooh fell to the

ground again! Christopher Robin and Pooh managed to escape from the angry bees by running away and hiding in a mud puddle.

But Pooh was not about to give up his hunt for honey! He went to Rabbit's house for lunch. Rabbit served him honey…and Pooh ate, and ate, and ate, ate, ate.

"I must be going now," Pooh finally said in a sticky voice. He started to climb out of the burrow's front door—and got stuck! Rabbit ran out his back door to find some help. Christopher Robin tried to pull Pooh out, but couldn't. Rabbit tried to push Pooh out, but couldn't.

"We shall have to wait for you to get thin again," Christopher Robin said. Rabbit tried to make the best of it, and decorated Pooh's backside with a frame, candles, and branches. But it all collapsed when Pooh sneezed. "Why did I *ever* invite that bear for lunch?" Rabbit sighed.

Day after day, Pooh waited to get thin. Rabbit made sure that no one fed the bear. Finally one morning, Pooh budged slightly! Christopher Robin, Owl, Kanga, Eeyore, Roo, and Gopher tugged and tugged while Rabbit pushed from inside his house.

POP! Out came Pooh. He sailed right over their heads and into a tree hollow— filled with honey. "Yum!" said Pooh happily.

Chapter 2: A Blustery Day

Several days later, Pooh set off to wish his friends a happy Windsday, because it was a blustery sort of day. First, he went to Piglet's house. Little Piglet was tossed around by the wind. Pooh caught him by a thread and flew him like a kite.

Clunk! Piglet and Pooh landed against Owl's window. Owl let them in. As Pooh snacked on honey, the house rocked back and forth from the blustery wind until— *CRASH!*—Owl's tree house fell. Now Owl's house was ruined.

"I'll find him a new place to live," Eeyore volunteered.

The blustery day turned into a blustery night. Pooh did not sleep very well. First, Tigger bounced by to visit. Then Pooh dreamed that dozens of heffalumps and woozles stole his honey. When he awoke, his house was filled with rain. The Hundred-Acre Wood was flooding!

The forest got floodier and floodier. Piglet had to abandon his home. He sailed off on a chair. Pooh couldn't help. He was stuck headfirst in a honeypot.

Only Christopher Robin's house was safe from the floods. Everyone gathered there. Owl spotted Piglet and Pooh floating downstream. Before Owl could help, the two friends sailed over a waterfall and into the river below!

Christopher Robin helped them to shore. He congratulated Pooh for rescuing Piglet, who was safe and dry in Pooh's honeypot. "I will give you a hero party," Christopher Robin said. Just then, Eeyore showed up. He had been looking for a new house for Owl. To everyone's surprise, the donkey led the way to…Piglet's house!

Piglet, however, was very kind—he let Owl have his grand house in the beech tree. Pooh told Piglet that he could move in with him. Then Christopher Robin made the party in honor of both Pooh and Piglet. "Hip, hip, Pooh-ray for Winnie the Pooh—and Piglet, too!" everyone cheered.

Chapter 3: Winnie the Pooh
and Tigger, Too

That winter, snow
fell heavily in the
Hundred-Acre Wood.
Tigger and Roo went
off to play. "Ice-skating
is what tiggers do best!"
Tigger said. He slid across the frozen pond,
crashed into Rabbit, and landed in a
snowbank. "Tiggers don't like ice-skating,"
Tigger declared.

He and Roo then climbed up a tree—
actually Tigger bounced
up—but then Tigger
was too scared to
come down!

Meanwhile, Piglet came across Pooh circling a nearby tree. "What are you doing?" Piglet asked his friend as he followed Pooh around the tree.

"Tracking!" said Pooh. "How mysterious—now there's a new set of tracks! Whatever made the first set has been joined by another animal!" So the two friends continued to walk and worry.

Then Pooh spotted something sitting way up in a tree. "It's a jagular!" Pooh said. Then Roo called out to them. "Oh, it's only Roo and Tigger!" Pooh said in relief.

Christopher Robin and the others came over and gathered at the foot of the tree. "We'll just have to get them down," Christopher Robin said. He held out his coat, and Kanga, Piglet, and Pooh held the other corners. "Jump, Roo!"

"Whee!" called Roo as he jumped safely into the coat. Finally, Tigger managed to jump, skid, and tumble down to the ground.

"No bouncing ever again!" scolded Rabbit. Tigger looked so sad! Everyone agreed that they liked the old bouncy Tigger better— even Rabbit said so! That made Tigger so happy he bounced. And so did they all.

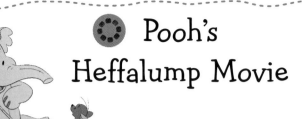

Pooh's Heffalump Movie

It was early one morning in the Hundred-Acre Wood. A loud trumpeting noise woke everyone.

"Bother!" groaned Pooh. Piglet stumbled out the door to see what it was. The noise bounced Tigger out of bed and across the room.

DISK 1
1

"Rabbit will know what to do," Piglet said. They all talked nervously about the terrible sound—all but Roo, who was chasing a butterfly nearby. That's when he noticed the ground was somehow different. Tigger thought it was a swimming pool. Eeyore came by and thought it was a crater. Only Roo realized it was an enormous footprint—but who could make a footprint that big?

"There's only one thing it could be—a heffalump!" said Rabbit. He and Tigger explained that a heffalump was big and wide…and very, very scary. "And they live right over there—in Heffalump Hollow!" Rabbit said, pointing to the nearby woods.

"Let's go get them!" Roo suggested. "It would be…an expotition!"

"It would be a first. The first heffalump expedition in history," Rabbit said.

Everyone gathered their equipment and met at the top of the hill. Roo brought some rope, and Rabbit tried to teach them how to lasso a heffalump. Roo was very good at it. But the others wouldn't let him join them because he was too young and might get hurt on the expotition.

So early the next morning, Roo set off on his own, armed with his rope. As he walked through Heffalump Hollow, something began to follow him. The first thing Roo noticed was that his lunch disappeared. "Is anyone there?" he called.

Suddenly, something brushed by him. "I tagged you—you're it!" said a laughing voice. "Don't you want to play?"

"I've got to go catch a heffalump!" Roo explained.

"You can catch me—*I'm* a heffalump!" declared the creature. His name was Lumpy. Roo was confused— Lumpy wasn't scary at all. But

Roo lassoed Lumpy anyway. "In the name of the Hundred-Acre Wood, I capture you!" Lumpy thought it was all a game. Soon

6 he was playfully dragging Roo around.

Then they heard a deeper trumpet sound. "My mummy is calling," cried Lumpy. "I have to go now!" he told Roo.

Roo tried to convince Lumpy to come visit his friends. He pulled on his rope and shouted, "Let's go!"

But Lumpy wouldn't budge. "Scary things live there," he said. "There's a stripy

7 thing that bounces, and a little pink monster that squeals. And there's the loud thing! It's got long ears and it yells at everybody!"

Roo gave a laugh. "That's just Tigger

and Piglet and Rabbit!" he explained. "My friends won't hurt you."

They went to Pooh's house, but Pooh wasn't home. They helped themselves to Pooh's honey before moving on to Rabbit's garden—and some watermelon. "I guess Pooh and Rabbit won't mind," said Roo. Soon he and his new friend were having the time of their lives together.

8

DISK 2

9 Meanwhile, the others had returned from their own hunting trip. "All in all, a successful heffalump expedition," said Rabbit proudly. "Just look around. You don't see any heffalumps, do you?"

Then he
stared in horror.
Heffalump footprints led
straight to Pooh's home! "It's an
invasion! They're all around us! We're
trapped!" they said in panic.

"That's it—we need traps!" cried
Rabbit. They set to work building traps.
Lumpy and Roo trotted along in the
Hundred-Acre Wood, tired but
happy, looking for Lumpy's
mother. They could hear her
in the distance, but they
couldn't find her.

"My mom will know what
to do!" Roo said. "Let's ask her."
Now Kanga, who hadn't seen her
son all day, was getting worried. "Roo?
Roo?" she called, looking everywhere.

10

"Have any of you seen Roo?" she asked the gang. "He should be home by now."

Just then, Roo and Lumpy appeared. "This is Lumpy," Roo told everyone. "He's a heffalump!"

"A real heffalump—and it's got Roo!" cried the others. Terrified, Lumpy ran off, missing most of the traps. Roo raced after him. He found the young heffalump in a bamboo cage, the only trap he didn't miss.

"You said they wouldn't be scary," sniffled Lumpy, as Roo freed him.

Kanga arrived in time to see Lumpy giving Roo a hug. But the others misunderstood. They thought Lumpy had captured Roo! "In the name of the Hundred-Acre Wood, we capture you!" they declared, lassoing Lumpy.

"You're scaring him!" cried Roo.

"Heffalumps aren't big and scary. They're just like us. Lumpy gets afraid, and he likes honey. He's even learning to bounce!"

Poor Lumpy backed away, fearful—and started sliding down a slope. Roo grabbed for him, but got thrown into the deadfall below! Lumpy raced to the edge to look for Roo.

"Mama?" Roo cried. He slid further. Kanga and Tigger tried to pull him out, but they weren't strong enough.

"Hold on, Roo!" called Lumpy. He trumpeted as loud as he could. "*Taroot!*"

"*Tooooot!*" came an answering trumpet.

"Mummy!" Lumpy cried with happiness.

Something came crashing out of the forest. "Heffridge Trumpler Brompet Heffalump the Fourth! Where have you been?" scolded Lumpy's mama.

"My friend Roo is in trouble! Can't you save him?" Lumpy pleaded.

Mama Heffalump went carefully. Finally she was able to snake her long trunk down and pluck Roo out.

She passed Roo to Kanga, who hugged him tightly.

"That's why the heffalump was in our wood, Rabbit. She was looking for her baby!" said Pooh.

Rabbit spoke to Lumpy. "Can you ever forgive us? We've acted very badly."

"That's okay, Longears," said Lumpy.

"Mama, can we please stay up just a bit longer?" Roo asked his mother.

"Pleeeeaaassee?" Lumpy asked, too.

The mothers agreed.

"So Roo captured the heffalump!" said Piglet, as Roo and Lumpy romped.

"Actually, it looks as if Lumpy has captured us," Pooh replied.